Stolen by Squat!

Hovering above Blork's space scooter was a huge spaceship. It was so big that if Blork had landed his scooter on *top* of it, the scooter would have looked like a ladybug sitting on a dinner plate.

A purple sucker-upper beam was coming down from the bottom of the spaceship. It had Blork's scooter. Slowly, slowly, the little scooter was being pulled into a big opening in the belly of the ship.

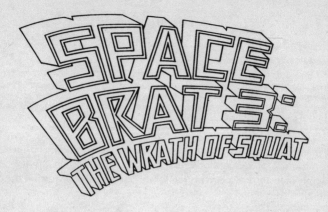

SPACE BRAT 3: THE WRATH OF SQUAT

BRUCE COVILLE

Interior illustrations by
Katherine Coville

A MINSTREL® BOOK

PUBLISHED BY POCKET BOOKS

New York   London   Toronto   Sydney   Tokyo   Singapore

For Pat MacDonald

This book is a work of fiction. Names, characters, places, and incidents are products of the author's imagination or are used fictitiously. Any resemblance to actual events or locales or persons, living or dead, is entirely coincidental.

A MINSTREL PAPERBACK *ORIGINAL*

 A Minstrel Book published by
POCKET BOOKS, a division of Simon & Schuster Inc.
1230 Avenue of the Americas, New York, NY 10020

Copyright © 1994 by Bruce Coville
Interior illustrations copyright © 1994 by Katherine Coville
Front cover illustration copyright © 1994 by Willardson & Associates

ISBN: 0-671-86844-6

First Minstrel Books paperback printing August 1994

10 9 8 7 6 5 4 3 2

A MINSTREL BOOK and colophon are registered trademarks
of Simon & Schuster Inc.

Printed in the U.S.A.

Contents

BIG NEWS!

Blork was mad at his desk. The math problem it had just given him was so hard it made his antennae ache.

Before he could even figure out how to start, the problem vanished. In its place glowed the face of Tayka Ledder, the school secretary.

"Blork!" she said loudly. "Report to the office at once! The principal wants to see you!"

The other kids began to snicker. Their teacher, Modra Ploogsik, rolled her eyes and sighed.

Blork groaned. He had spent half his life being sent to the office—first for things he hadn't even done, later for rotten things that he *had* done. Now that everyone had decided he was a hero instead of the worst brat on the Planet Splat, he had hoped the office visits would stop.

"Blork's in *trou*-ble, Blork's in *trou*-ble," sang Appus Meko as Blork trudged out of the room.

This made Blork even more nervous. Appus Meko had a talent for making mischief and getting Blork blamed for it. Had his enemy struck again?

"I hope I don't get sent to the Big Black Pit," Blork muttered as he trudged along the hall. "I hate it when that happens." He paused. "Maybe they wouldn't do that to someone who saved the city from getting shrunk," he said, feeling more hopeful.

Tayka Ledder smiled as Blork came through the door.

He flinched. That smile was not a good sign. Back in his brat days, Blork had given the secretary some candy that turned her teeth blue for two days. After that, she hardly ever smiled when she saw him—unless he was about to get in trouble. Then she always looked very happy.

"He's waiting for you," said Tayka Ledder, pointing to the principal's door.

Blork's antennae drooped. He trudged through the office door.

The principal, Yellin Bello, was standing by his desk. He was playing with an atomic yo-yo he had taken away from one of the kids earlier that day. "Glad to see you, Space Brat," he said happily.

"Space Brat" was the name the newsies had given Blork after his first adventure. Yellin Bello liked the attention the story had brought to the school, and now he always called Blork by that name.

"Sit down, sit down!" said the principal, pointing to a chair.

"Am I in trouble?" Blork asked, feeling confused.

"Trouble? Hardly! Wait until I tell you the news!"

School was over by the time Blork left the office. He couldn't wait to tell the others what had happened.

He ran to his space scooter, which the Big Boss of Splat had given him as a reward for saving the city.

"Space Brat and away!" he cried, firing up the engine. Then he zoomed into the sky and headed for the Block 78 Child House.

Moomie Peevik was standing out front when he landed. Blork was glad. Moomie Peevik was sort of his best friend, even if she was a girl.

The first thing Blork heard when he got out of the space scooter was a squeaky voice crying, "Aroonga Boonga Boonga!"

The voice belonged to Blabber, Moomie Peevik's pet fuzzygrumper. Blabber was running in circles around a giant purple animal with six legs. The purple animal was a poodnoobie. It was named Lunk, and it was Blork's pet. Blork loved Lunk, who was very sweet, and very stupid.

"Aroonga Boonga Boonga!" cried Blabber again, running even faster.

Lunk twirled around, trying to keep the fuzzygrumper in sight.

Blork frowned. Lunk was trying to keep Blabber in sight because he was afraid the fuzzygrumper might bite him in a tender place. Blork knew Lunk would soon be dizzy from trying to keep up with him. The fuzzygrumper knew this, too. He thought it was fun to watch Lunk stagger around with his eyes going in circles.

"Make Blabber stop!" said Blork. "Lunk might throw up."

Poodnoobies weigh about three hundred

5

and fifty pounds and eat lots of strange stuff, so making them barf is a bad idea.

Moomie Peevik wiggled her antennae in annoyance. "Blabber is just having fun!"

"He's having fun like Appus Meko has fun," replied Blork. He was surprised Moomie Peevik would think it was all right for Blabber to pick on Lunk. She was usually very sensitive to animals.

Moomie Peevik frowned. She didn't like having her pet compared to someone who made trouble just for the fun of it. But she knew Blork was right. "Come here, Blabber," she said.

Squawking with delight, the fuzzygrumper ran to Moomie Peevik and leaped into her arms.

Lunk burped with relief. Then his eyes went around in circles and he fell over. He was drooling, but that didn't mean anything. He drooled a lot.

"Are you all right, boy?" asked Blork, squatting down to pat the poodnoobie's head.

Lunk stuck out his middle tongue—

poodnoobies have three—and licked Blork's face.

"He's fine," said Blork, wiping away the slobber. Turning to Moomie Peevik, he said, "Guess what? I'm going to the Galactic Celebration!"

The Galactic Celebration was the biggest party in history. All the kids were dying to go, but none of them ever thought they would actually have a chance.

"Don't lie, Blork," said Moomie Peevik. "It's not nice."

"I'm not lying!" shouted Blork. "I'm really going! The Grand High Fimbul wants to give me a medal for stopping my evil twin from shrinking the city."

"Blork, that's wonderful! Everyone in the galaxy will know who you are."

Suddenly Moomie Peevik's face got very serious. Her brow wrinkled and her antennae drooped.

"What's the matter?" asked Blork.

Moomie Peevik sighed. "What will Appus Meko do when he hears about this?"

"When I hear about what?" asked Appus

Meko, who had just come out of the Child House.

"I'm getting a medal!" said Blork happily.

"For what? Being the biggest jerk on the planet?"

Blork started to tremble. He started to shake. He could feel the old tantrum feelings starting to bubble inside him.

Stop! he told himself. *That's just what Appus Meko wants.*

Blork was right about that much. Appus Meko had loved goading Blork into the tantrums that had earned him the title "Biggest Brat on the Planet Splat." When Blork had learned to stop having tantrums it drove Appus Meko crazy. He was always trying to make Blork blow up again.

Appus Meko wasn't the only one upset about Blork's good news. Thousands of light-years away, on the Planet of Cranky People, someone else had found out that Blork was getting a medal—someone who was so mad at Blork that the very mention of his name made smoke come out of his ears.

That someone was Blork's old enemy, Squat. When he heard the news about the medal, Squat threw himself out of his chair and began to roll around on the floor, kicking and screaming. "I can't stand it!" he shrieked. *"I can't stand it!"*

Since Blork himself had taught Squat how to throw a tantrum, he was very good at it. (Though not as good as Blork, of course.)

When Squat had finished, he lay on his back, staring at the ceiling. Then he began to laugh—a cruel, wicked laugh.

If Blork had known what Squat was thinking, he would have stopped worrying about Appus Meko.

But he didn't know, of course.

So he had no idea of the terrible thing Squat had decided to do.

2

BIG
THINGS

The next few weeks were not easy for Blork.

For one thing, he was so excited about going to the Galactic Celebration that he couldn't sleep at night.

For another thing, the newsies were constantly after him. Stories about "The Kid Known as Space Brat" were showing up everywhere.

For a third thing, Appus Meko was driving him nuts.

"He's just jealous because of all the news stories," whispered Moomie Peevik. She was sitting next to Blork as he struggled to open his backpack, which Appus Meko had electro-zapped shut.

When Blork finally got the backpack open, he found a note inside.

BLORK IS A ROTTEN EGG! it said in big, thick letters. (Children on Splat are hatched instead of being born, so this is one of the worst insults anyone can make.)

Blork began to tremble. The old tantrum feeling began bubbling inside him.

"Take a deep breath," whispered Moomie Peevik.

Blork needed *ten* deep breaths to get calmed down again.

He thought about going to Modra Ploog-sik to complain. But since he had no way to prove it was Appus Meko doing these things, he kept his mouth shut.

When Blork didn't blow up after two days of insults and tricks, Appus Meko opened a new line of attack. Instead of doing things to Blork, he started doing things to other people and trying to get Blork blamed for them. But in the same way that when Blork was a brat he got blamed for everything, now that he was a hero he didn't get blamed for anything.

This was just as well, since he wasn't actually doing anything. But Appus Meko was so good at making *himself* look innocent that other kids were getting blamed for his pranks.

For example, when Appus Meko fiddled with the computer and made Modra Ploogsik's desk burp all day long, it was Murgo who got sent to the Whacking Room.

When he put hot sauce in the fried skunjies and scalded everyone's tonsils, it was Plonk who had to spend five days cleaning the kitchen with a toothbrush and a pair of tweezers.

And when he put Mimsy Borogrove's pet gitzels in the Fluff-O-Matic Pillow Poofer and they came out looking like tiny clouds with eyes, it was Lakka who had to write a five-hundred-page essay on why we should be kind to animals.

Everyone knew who the real troublemaker was. But no one could prove it.

Finally Murgo and some of the others came to Blork to complain.

"If you're such a hero, why can't you make Appus Meko stop causing so much trouble?" asked Brillig.

"We're all afraid of what he'll do next," said Lakka.

"The Childkeeper is about to have a nervous breakdown," added Bob the Foreign Student. "It keeps rolling around in circles beeping, 'Where did I go wrong? Where did I go wrong?'"

"You've got to do something, Blork!" they all cried.

Blork sighed. He hadn't done a single thing wrong. He hadn't even been blamed for anything. And he was *still* in trouble. Some hero.

That night he slipped out of bed. With Lunk at his side, he left the Block 78 Child House and climbed into his space scooter.

"Space Brat and away!" he yelled as he pushed the Zoomstick.

They soared into the stratosphere.

Lunk looked out the window. He started

to drool. (Not because he was afraid. He just liked to drool.)

Blork flew all the way to the other side of the Planet Splat. It was daytime on that side of the world, of course. He landed in the Unexplored Zone. This was where he had had his first adventure. It was also where he had learned not to have tantrums.

"Hello!" he called, climbing out of the ship. "Anyone home?"

Some big Things came out of the bushes. They were about three times as tall as Blork. They had tiny eyes, thick brows, pebbly gray-green skin, and broad shoulders. Their arms hung down below their knees.

"Blork!" they cried happily. "You have come back!"

They had voices like small earthquakes, and they spoke in Thing-talk. Blork could understand them because he had learned their language when the Mighty Squat had held him prisoner.

"I am just here for a visit," said Blork. "I wanted to get away from home for a little while."

The Things decided to have a welcome-back picnic. They made huge piles of purple fruit. Everyone sat down. The Chief Thing sang a thank-you song. Then everyone had a big feed.

Later, Blork told the Things everything that had happened to him since he had helped them get rid of Squat. He told them how hard it had been to change his reputation when people still expected him to be a giant brat. He told them how he had accidentally made an evil twin of himself named Krolb, who had almost shrunk the entire city. Finally he told them about Appus Meko and his rotten tricks.

The Things shook their heads and made clucking noises.

"Maybe you should give him a kick in the pants," said one of them. (This was one of the ways the Things had gotten Blork to stop being such a brat.)

It was Blork's turn to shake his head. "I would only get in trouble."

The Things scratched their noses, which was what they did when something didn't make sense to them.

"Bring him here, and we will kick him in the pants for you," offered another Thing cheerfully.

Blork liked that idea. However, he was pretty sure it would make the Childkeeper very angry.

"I don't think so," he said sadly.

It began to get dark—which meant it would be getting light on the other side of Splat. It was time for Blork to fly home.

"Come on, boy," he said to Lunk. "Let's go."

Lunk had eaten so much that he couldn't walk. The Things had to carry him to the space scooter.

"Space Brat and away!" cried Blork, once Lunk was on board. He pushed the zoomstick. The Things had to give the scooter a little push because of Lunk's extra weight, but soon it was soaring into the stratosphere.

Some of the kids were already outside when Blork got home. He could see Moomie Peevik and Appus Meko having an argument. Blabber was running around them, flapping his tongue and waving his arms.

Blork headed toward them, planning to set the space scooter down nearby so he could help Moomie Peevik.

Suddenly a huge shadow covered the scooter. Then a beam of purple light surrounded it.

The scooter stopped going forward. It began to float upward.

Moomie Peevik and Appus Meko had stopped fighting. They were looking up. They looked terrified.

Blork looked up, too, through the top of the scooter.

"Uh-oh," he said to Lunk. "We're in big trouble."

3

BIG TRIP

A huge spaceship was hovering above Blork's scooter. It was so big that if Blork had landed his scooter on *top* of it, the scooter would have looked like a ladybug sitting on a dinner plate.

A purple sucker-upper beam was shining from the bottom of the spaceship. It had Blork's scooter. Slowly, slowly, he was being pulled into an opening in the belly of the ship.

Blork hit the zoomstick as hard as he could. The scooter quivered. Its engine began to whine. But it could not break free of the beam.

Blork could hear the other kids shouting and screaming. He looked down. They were all pointing at the big ship—all except Moomie Peevik and Appus Meko. They had been right below him when the big ship started to pull him up. Now they were floating in mid-air. Like Blork, they had been caught in the sucker-upper beam!

Blork hit the zoom-stick again. The engine screamed. A burning smell filled the cabin. He pulled the stick back. No

sense in destroying the engine. They might need it later.

Soon Blork was in the belly of the giant ship. The only light came from the open door beneath them. Then that door closed and everything went black.

Blork felt a coldness in his heart.

Lunk began to whine.

The space scooter was lowered slowly to the floor.

Blork opened the top of the scooter and stuck out his head. "Anyone here?" he called.

"Me!" cried Moomie Peevik from somewhere nearby.

"Aaaahhh!" screamed Appus Meko. "Get me out of here! Get me out of here!"

"Aroonga Boonga Boonga!" shrieked Blabber.

Lunk burped.

"Blork, what's going on?" asked Moomie Peevik.

"I don't know!" said Blork.

"Aaaahhh!" cried Appus Meko again. "We're all going to die. We're all going to die!"

"Shut up," said Blork and Moomie Peevik.

Suddenly the lights came on. Blork blinked for a moment. When his eyes got used to the light, he looked around. He swallowed hard and thought, *Maybe we are going to die.*

At the top of the huge chamber into which they had been drawn was a little platform. Standing on the platform was a short man. A cruel expression twisted his face.

"Squat!" cried Blork.

"Why?" asked Moomie Peevik.

Appus Meko didn't bother to ask why. He just hunkered down, crying, "Don't let me die, don't let me die!"

"I don't mean squat," said Blork. "I mean *Squat!* That's who has us. There he is, up there!"

"Quiet, you fool!" roared Squat. "Fall down in fear! It is time for you to tremble before the wrath of Squat!"

"Blow it out your nose!" cried Blork. The tantrum feeling was rumbling deep inside him, but he pushed it down. A tantrum would not do any good right now. It would only make Squat throw a tantrum, too.

23

"Laugh now!" cried Squat. "You won't be laughing long!"

"I'm not laughing!" cried Appus Meko. "I'm not laughing! Let me go and I'll never laugh again."

"Shut up," said Blork, Moomie Peevik, and Squat, all at the same time.

Then Squat turned out the lights. They heard a nasty laugh, followed by the sound of the door hissing shut.

"Now see what you've done, Blork!" yelled Appus Meko.

"He didn't do anything," said Moomie Peevik. "Stop whining, or when we get back I'll tell all the other kids what a pazootie you are."

Pazooties were furry little animals that sometimes got so frightened their tails fell off.

"When we get back?" cried Appus Meko. "What makes you think we'll ever get back?" Suddenly he started to scream again. "What's that? *WHAT'S THAT?*"

"What's what?" cried Blork and Moomie Peevik.

"Something is trying to eat me!"

Blork felt a twinge of fear. Had Squat locked them in the dark with some horrible creature that ate Splatoonians?

Appus Meko continued to scream.

Suddenly Blork figured out what was going on. "Blabber!" he called. "Blabber, come here."

Little feet began to patter in his direction. "Aroonga?" asked a familiar voice.

"It stopped!" said Appus Meko.

"Of course it stopped," said Moomie Peevik. "It was only Blabber."

"I hate that fuzzygrumper," muttered Appus Meko.

"What you hate isn't the point," said Blork. "The point is, we have to figure out what to do next."

But the truth was, there was nothing to do but wait . . . and wait . . . and wait . . . and *wait*.

After a while Blork heard a deep rumbling noise.

"What's that?" cried Appus Meko.

"Lunk's stomach," said Blork. "I think he's getting hungry."

Though he didn't say it, this made Blork nervous. He and Lunk loved each other very much. But it was never a good idea to be stuck in the dark with a starving poodnoobie.

Suddenly a weird ringing noise filled the darkness. Blork felt as if he were being pulled inside out. Purple lights flashed inside his head.

"What is it?" cried Moomie Peevik. "What's happening? I never felt aaaaanythiiii-innnggg liiike iiiiiiiit-t-t-t."

Blork had never felt anything like it, either. But he had read about it.

"Iiiiit-t-t's aaaaaaaa spaaaaaaace shiiiiiffffft-t-t!" he said. "Weeeeeeee'reeee juuumpii-innnnnnggg acrooooossssss—"

Suddenly everything changed.

"—the stars," he finished.

"A space shift," whispered Appus Meko in awe. "We could be anywhere in the galaxy now. We could be thousands of light-years from home!"

Suddenly Squat's voice came blasting through the darkness. "You are now thousands of light-years from home. At least, from *your* home. We're about to land on my home, the Planet Snarf—otherwise known as 'The Planet of Cranky People.'"

27

"Sounds great," moaned Moomie Peevik.

"It's terrible!" laughed Squat. "And guess who runs it."

Blork had a feeling he knew the answer, but he refused to give Squat the satisfaction of saying it.

"I do!" bellowed Squat. "And guess why. Give up? The answer is simple. Because I have the greatest tantrums on the planet. My tantrums are so fantastic that they made me the Emperor of Snarf! Only one person has ever defeated me, and it is time for that person to pay the price for squelching Squat!"

Then Squat began to laugh—a long, terrible laugh that echoed through the darkness.

When the laughter died away, the darkness was silent once more, except for Lunk's stomach, and Appus Meko's sniveling.

"Oh, stop it," said Moomie Peevik. "Squat doesn't want you. Blork's the one . . ."

Her voice trailed off as a huge viewscreen lit up on one side of their prison.

"Behold the end of your journey," said their captor. "Behold: *Castle Squat!*"

On the screen loomed the biggest, scariest

place Blork had ever seen. Castle Squat rose from the top of a high, rocky hill. Its huge towers stretched into the dark sky. Big creatures with pointy wings circled the towers. Streaks of lightning flashed around them.

"Welcome home!" cried Squat happily.

4

BIG
TROUBLE

Through the view screen they saw a huge door open in the side of the mountain. As the ship flew through the door, the screen went blank.

They were left in darkness again until Squat reappeared on the little platform. He had a ray gun in each hand and three more strapped around his waist.

The platform slid down to where Blork and the others stood waiting.

"Right, then," said Squat, stepping off. "Out you go!"

"Wow," whispered Moomie Peevik. "I had no idea he was so short."

"Shut up!" roared Squat, blasting a ray of hot red light into the floor in front of Moomie Peevik's feet.

Blabber yelped and leaped into Moomie Peevik's arms. Appus Meko screamed and jumped, too, but nobody caught him.

"You rotten bully!" cried Moomie Peevik. "You scared Blabber."

"We're going to die, I know we're going to die," whined Appus Meko, who was now lying on the floor.

"Shut up!" shouted Blork, Moomie Peevik, and Squat.

A door opened in the side of the ship.

"Out you go," said Squat again, waving his ray gun.

The five Splatoonians walked through the door. They found themselves in a big cave. Flickering torches cast a dim glow over everything. Strange creatures hung from the ceiling and crawled along the walls. Dark holes showed where passages wound into the mountainside.

"Ah, home, sweet home," said Squat.

"How come you use torches instead of electricity?" asked Moomie Peevik.

"I like to play with fire," said Squat.

He pushed a button on the wall. A dozen tall creatures scuttled from one of the passages. They had six arms and long orange hair. They looked like human spiders wearing wigs.

"Yes, Master?" asked one of them. Its voice sounded juicy, as if it had a mouthful of spit.

"Take my guests to the room we prepared for them," said Squat.

When Squat called them "guests," Blork wondered if things might not be as bad as he had feared.

But Squat was not done. "You know the ones I mean," he continued. "The ones deep in the dungeons." He laughed. Then he turned to Blork and the others and added, "I'll meet you there. *I'm* taking the elevator."

Squat kept his ray gun handy while the spider-people picked up Blork and popped

him into a bag. Pop! into another bag went Appus Meko. Moomie Peevik was next, and then Blabber. The only one they did not pop into a bag was Lunk, who would not have fit even if they had tried. It didn't matter. Wherever they took Blork, Lunk would follow.

Blork did not like being in the bag. But he had a feeling that when Squat finally told them his plans, being in the bag might seem like a good idea. It would almost certainly be better than whatever Squat had in mind.

The spider-people sang a nasty, whiny song as they made the long trip into the mountain beneath Castle Squat:

> *"Down to the darkness, down to the deep,*
> *Into the heart of the mountain we creep;*
> *Down to the terror, down to the fear,*
> *Away from there and into here!"*

They sang this song so many times that Blork finally shouted, "If you don't shut up I'm going to barf!"

"Quiet in the bag! Quiet in the bag!" yelled one of the spider-people. Then it shook the bag so hard Blork was afraid his teeth would come loose.

Blork dug his fingers into his ears to shut out the singing. He could still hear it. Finally the creatures sang a last verse. On "Away from there and into *here!*" they dropped their bags onto a hard floor.

"Let them out," said Squat.

Someone picked up the end of Blork's bag and shook it. Blork rolled out onto the floor. Moomie Peevik, Appus Meko, and Blabber came out of their bags in the same way.

Lunk ran over and licked Blork's face with his softest tongue, the one he used whenever he was worried about Blork.

"Why didn't you just take us on the elevator with you?" asked Blork, wiping the poodnoobie slobber from his cheek.

"The Mighty Squat does not share!" chanted all the spider-people.

Blork started to say something, but stopped. The place they were in was not anything like he had expected. Instead of a stony cell with damp walls and torchlight, it was a laboratory filled with strange equipment.

In the center of the lab stood two metal tables. Between the tables was a tall man with olive green skin. A patch of bright red hair sprouted from the top of his head.

"This is Dr. Pimento," said Squat. "He will be our host for tonight's experiment."

"What experiment is that?" asked Blork.

"He's a mad scientist!" cried Appus Meko. "We're all going to die!"

"My goodness, you don't have much faith in me, do you?" asked Dr. Pimento in a squeaky voice. He looked sad, and his eyes got so big that they took up almost half his face.

"What exactly is this experiment?" asked Blork again.

"Oh, it's very interesting," said Dr. Pimento. He was so excited that he started to drool, which made him seem a little like Lunk. "I'm going to do an electronic brain transplant!"

"A *what*?" asked Moomie Peevik.

Dr. Pimento's eyes got even bigger, which Blork would have thought was impossible. He rubbed his hands together eagerly. "I am going to use my electro-frammistat to transfer one person's experiences and personality into someone else's skull!"

Blork swallowed. His skin turned a very pale shade of green.

"And guess whose brain is going where?" asked Squat, chuckling evilly.

Blork looked around. That Squat was going to use him for the experiment, he had no doubt. The question was, who was he going to be forced to swap brains with?

Appus Meko? What a revolting development that would be!

Moomie Peevik? Even Squat wouldn't put

his brain into a girl's body. *Or would he?* Blork wondered in terror.

Maybe it would be with one of the spider-people. Blork looked at them, and shivered at the thought.

"Why don't you tell me and get it over with?" he cried at last.

"Because I'm enjoying the suspense," said Squat.

"Tell me!" shrieked Blork.

Squat laughed. "I see the suspense has reached the proper level. All right, I'll answer your question. Your brain is going . . . there!"

Blork gasped. Squat was pointing at Lunk!

"Of course, we'll have to store Lunk's brain in your head," continued Squat happily. "After all, we have to do *something* with it."

"Putting Blork's brain into that poodnoobie's body is cruel and terrible," said Appus Meko. "No one should treat a poodnoobie like that!"

"I am cruel and terrible!" cried Squat, firing his ray gun at a little creature crawling across the ceiling. He opened his mouth and caught the creature as it fell. "That's why I

came up with this plan in the first place," he added.

"You shouldn't talk with your mouth full," said Moomie Peevik politely. She didn't mention the fact that the creature's legs were still sticking out between Squat's lips.

"Quiet, twit, or you're next!" roared Squat. Waving his ray gun, he said, "Onto the table, Mr. Hero-of-the-Galaxy."

Blork didn't want to get onto the table. But as long as Squat had the ray gun, he didn't see that he had much choice.

He wondered what a real hero would do in this situation.

Gritting his teeth, he climbed onto the metal table. It was cold.

"A little to the left, please," said Dr. Pimento. He strapped Blork down and put a metal helmet onto his head. "That's fine. Now you, big boy," he said, turning to Lunk and gesturing to the other table.

Lunk whined and backed away.

"Tell him to get up there!" demanded Squat.

"Climb onto the table, boy," said Blork.

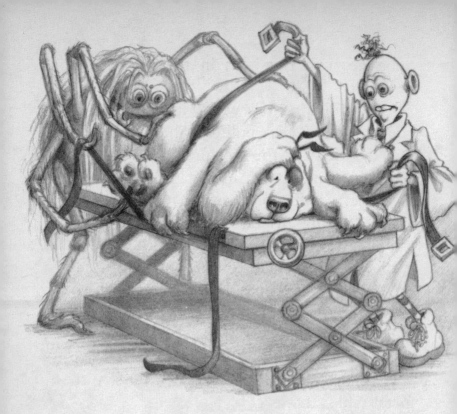

Quaking and whining, Lunk climbed onto the table. It took Dr. Pimento longer to strap Lunk down, and he had to have help from several of the spider-people. Once Lunk was securely in place, they put another metal helmet on his head.

"At last!" cried Squat. "The day of vengeance has arrived! Dr. Pimento, prepare for the countdown!"

"All systems go!" said Dr. Pimento, stepping to the control panel.

"Then prepare for brain blast!" roared Squat. "Ten, nine, eight . . ."

"Can we talk about this?" asked Blork.

". . . seven, six, five . . ."

"Really, I think it's a terrible idea."

". . . four, three, two . . ."

"Stop!" cried Moomie Peevik. She ran toward Dr. Pimento. Three of the spider-people caught her and lifted her off the ground.

"ONE!" screamed Squat.

Dr. Pimento pulled the switch.

5

BIG SWITCH

A crackling, buzzing sound filled the secret laboratory. Sparks shot from wire to wire. The sound got louder. Soon it changed to a high-pitched whine. And still it was getting louder, *louder*, LOUDER.

Blork began to twitch.

A terrible burning smell filled the air.

Strange noises started coming from his mouth, and then from his ears.

"This is the most fun I've had in years!" screamed Squat.

The lights flickered on and off. A loud BANG! filled the room. Everything went black and silent.

"Ooops!" said Dr. Pimento. "I pushed the wrong lever."

"Fix it, you fool!" cried Squat. "The rest of you—freeze where you are!"

"Got it!" cried Dr. Pimento. After a moment the lights came back on. The doctor's eyes shrank to the size of buttons.

"Unstrap them," ordered Squat.

Six spider-people scrambled to each table. They undid the straps that held Blork and Lunk in place.

Blork sat on the edge of his table and moaned. After a moment, he tried to stand.

 That was when he realized that he had six legs; six furry *purple* legs, to be precise. "Ack gack glag urf!" he said. The sounds came from deep in his throat.

"He's trying to talk!" said Moomie Peevik, who was looking at him with wide and horrified eyes.

"Success!" cried Dr. Pimento joyfully. He began to hug himself. "Oooh, I am *such* a genius!"

"Congratulations," said Squat. "Now I want you to start working on teaching the new Blork how to walk."

At the words "the new Blork," Blork looked at the other table. To his horror, he saw *himself* sitting there. Only it wasn't really him, of course. It was his body with Lunk's personality inside. As usual, Lunk was drooling and looking confused—which meant that Blork's *body* was drooling and looking confused.

As Blork watched, his body got down on all fours and began to scramble around. Its head examined its middle, as if looking for its missing legs. Then it spotted him and yelped in fear.

I know just how you feel, boy, thought Blork.

Finally the Splatoonian body with the poodnoobian brain scurried over and hid its face against Moomie Peevik's knees.

Appus Meko started to laugh. "This is pretty cool," he said to Squat. "I like the way you think."

Blork wanted to go comfort Lunk. He climbed off the table. But he wasn't used to having six legs. After two steps his feet got tangled together and he fell on his face.

This made Appus Meko laugh so hard that he fell over, too.

From where he lay on his side, Blork tried to say, "Don't worry, Lunk. We'll get out of this somehow."

All that came out of his mouth were some noises that sounded like a poodnoobie trying not to lose its lunch.

Moomie Peevik ran over and patted Blork on his furry purple head. "Are you all right?" she asked.

"Ark! Gaggle! Rrrnch!" replied Blork. All three of his tongues flopped out of his mouth.

"Probably not easy to talk with that many tongues," said Appus Meko cheerfully.

"Take them to their cells," said Squat. "We'll start training the new Blork tomorrow."

"Training him for what?" asked Dr. Pimento.

Squat began to laugh. "We're going to send this poodnoobie-brained boy to the Galactic Celebration." Turning to Blork, he added, "Now do you see the genius of my plan? When your body goes to the Galactic Celebration to get your award, *the entire galaxy is going to think that you are a slobbering, drooling fool!* What embarrassment. What humiliation. What joy!"

"What a what *what?*" cried Dr. Pimento, his eyes getting big again.

"Silence!" roared Squat. "I want to savor this moment. It is a lesson for all who dare risk the wrath of Squat!" He closed his eyes and smiled. "Enough savoring," he said after less than three seconds. "Spider-people, take them away!"

The spider people grabbed Squat's prisoners and put them back into the bags—

all except Blork. Now that he was in Lunk's body, he was too big for that. But since he had not yet learned to control his new body, he could not follow on his own, either. After much fussing, the spider-people tied his feet together. Then they struck a pole through his legs. Three spider-people got on each end of the pole and picked him up.

This time Blork could see where they were going (though everything was upside down, of course). After he had seen a little bit, he decided he might rather be blindfolded. The twisty tunnels they traveled through were lit only by the spider-people's torches. When they passed openings into other tunnels, Blork saw big eyes watching from the darkness.

The eyes made him shiver.

Finally they came to a big cell. It had one tiny light in the ceiling. The spider-people locked everyone except Lunk inside.

"Good-bye!" they said in their juicy voices. "Good-bye!"

Still holding the bag with Lunk's brain and

Blork's body, they disappeared into the darkness.

Blork groaned and flopped onto the floor. Then he covered his head with four of his purple paws.

The spider-people brought food and water every day. But they would not answer any questions.

For the first two weeks Blork did not have much luck using Lunk's body. Whenever he tried to walk, his feet tangled together and he fell on his face. He had to get around by crawling.

He did discover one good thing about being in Lunk's body: He could make amazingly loud burps. In fact, if he waited until

Appus Meko was asleep, he could creep over to his enemy's ear and burp so loudly it would make him jump and scream.

After the third time Blork played Burp-Alarm-Clock, Appus Meko stopped teasing him. So Blork stopped doing it.

"Can you make your burps into sounds?" asked Moomie Peevik. "If you could, you might be able to talk that way."

Blork thought it was an interesting idea. He started to practice. It was hard, but it gave him something to do.

To his surprise, he found that learning something new was a good way to stop thinking about his problems.

Two weeks after Blork started to practice burp-talking the spider-people returned Lunk to the cell. By now he could walk standing up. But he still drooled a lot, and he kept licking things, like the wall and the floor.

"Stop that!" burped Blork, who was disgusted to see his body doing such things.

Lunk's eyes got wide. Hearing a voice come out of his old body made him so confused he walked into a wall and got a big bump right in the middle of his green face. It made him look a little like Bob the Foreign Student.

"I have a plan," said Moomie Peevik. "If we could make friends with one of the spider-people, maybe we could convince it to help us."

"Just like a girl," sneered Appus Meko.

Blork, who by this time had much better control of his body, walked over to Appus Meko and sat on him. "Come here, Blabber," he burped.

Blabber ran over and began to lick Appus Meko's face (which was all that was sticking out from under Blork's poodnoobian body).

"Help, help!" cried Appus Meko in a teeny, tiny voice. "Let me up!"

"Not until you promise to act nicer," said Moomie Peevik.

"I promise! I promise!"

"Let him up, Blork," said Moomie Peevik.

Blork wasn't sure this was a good idea. But he stood up anyway. He could always sit on Appus Meko again later if he needed to.

Now I know two good things about being a poodnoobie, he thought.

They decided they would try to make friends with the next spider-person who came to feed them. But to their surprise, their next visitor was someone else altogether.

"What are *you* doing here?" burped Blork angrily.

6

BIG TANTRUM

It was Dr. Pimento. He was carrying a torch, and he looked very surprised.

"I didn't know you could talk," he said to Blork. "That's marvelous!"

Blork waddled over to Dr. Pimento. He was about to sit on him when the scientist said, "Wait! I came to get you out of here."

"What do you mean?" burped Blork.

Dr. Pimento began to sniffle. Red tears leaked out of his big eyes. "I am so ashamed. All I wanted to do was try my experiment. I was planning to switch your brain back into your own body the same day. I didn't know Squat was planning to make you *stay* this way until I heard him say so the day I pulled the switch on you. I have been trying to get down here for the last four weeks. I want to take you back to the lab and make things right."

I'm glad I spent so much time practicing using this body, thought Blork as Dr. Pimento hustled them out of the cell.

They hadn't gone far when one of the spider-people came scuttling out of a side tunnel. "Eeeep!" it cried when it saw them. "Eeeep! Eeeep!"

Then it ran in the other direction.

"We scared him off!" burped Blork.

He had burped too soon. A siren began to howl.

"Prisoners are escaping! Prisoners are escaping!" shrieked a loudspeaker.

"Uh-oh," said Dr. Pimento. "He wasn't as scared as we thought. We won't be able to go to the lab now. We'll have to run for it."

"But how will I turn back?" burped Blork.

54

"We'll worry about that later," said Dr. Pimento. "If—"

Before he could finish, they heard hundreds of feet scuttling toward them.

"There they are!" cried a spider-person. *"Catch them!"*

"Aaaaahhh! We're all going to die, we're all going to die!" screamed Appus Meko.

"Not necessarily," whispered Dr. Pimento. "Follow me. I know a secret way out!"

They began to run. Dr. Pimento led the way, followed by Moomie Peevik and Blabber, then Appus Meko, and finally Blork and Lunk, each still in the wrong body.

They ran for a long time. Sometimes they heard spider-people behind them. Then they would run faster.

After a while the sounds of pursuit faded. Soon after, they came to a place where a ladder went up the wall.

"This way," said Dr. Pimento, starting up the ladder.

The ladder went straight up for a long way. This part of the trip was especially hard for Blork. Poodnoobie bodies are not built for climbing ladders. Nor was the rocky tunnel built for a poodnoobie's body. He kept getting stuck and had to pull and pull to get his big purple butt through tight places. The only good thing was that he was never in danger of falling. The tunnel was so narrow it would stop him before he went very far.

At last Dr. Pimento opened a trap door.

When they climbed out, they were in the middle of a crowded city. The gloomy buildings were small, pointed, and dark. The street signs said things like HONK LOUDER and NO SMILING and LAUGHERS WILL BE PERSECUTED.

Blork had never seen so many different kinds of people. There were tall ones and short ones, fat ones and skinny ones, pink, purple, green, blue, and red ones; people with stripes and people with spots; people who had arms and people who had tentacles; people with one eye, two eyes, three eyes, and more, sometimes right in their heads, sometimes on stalks.

These different people all had one thing in common: Every one of them looked incredibly cranky. They scurried along with big frowns on their faces, glancing suspiciously to the left and the right, as if each thought ev-

eryone else was trying to rob him. Everyone was shoving and pushing and calling names.

Not one of them talked to Blork and the others.

"This is the crankiest place I've ever seen," whispered Moomie Peevik.

"Of course it is," said Dr. Pimento. "Cranky people come from all over the galaxy to live on Snarf. They feel more at home here. I used to fit right in myself until one day when I was fooling around with my brain. I accidentally changed a few connections and somehow made myself pretty cheerful! They were going to throw me off the planet, but Squat decided he would put up with me for the sake of my inventions. I always—"

"We can't just stand here talking!" interrupted Appus Meko. "Squat is bound to send out a search party. We have to hide."

"I hate it when you make sense," burped Blork.

"It won't be easy to find a place to hide," said Dr. Pimento.

"Why not?" asked Moomie Peevik.

"Watch," said Dr. Pimento.

He walked up to a tall pink person who was grumping along the street. "Excuse me, sir," he said. "We are—"

"Leave me alone!" growled the pink person. He gave Dr. Pimento a shove and stalked away without looking back.

It was the same everywhere they went. People growled at them, cursed them, slammed doors in their faces. No one would help them.

Blork was getting more and more frustrated. "These people would step on a gitzel," he burped, starting to shake. "They'd spit in their leftovers rather than let you eat them. They wouldn't give you a drink if they were up to their necks in water. They wouldn't—"

"Blork," said Moomie Peevik. "Be careful. . . ."

"Go for it, Blorkie," said Appus Meko. "Let 'er rip."

Before anything could happen, a hovercar landed in front of them. Another landed behind them. Soon five others had landed. Squat climbed out of the first car. Dozens of spider-people clambered out after him.

"Did you really think you could escape the wrath of Squat?" he asked with a sneer.

"It was worth a try," said Moomie Peevik.

"Silence, female!" roared Squat. He turned to the spider-people. "Pack them up," he ordered. "When we go back to the castle, *everyone* gets a brain transplant!"

A crowd of cranky people had gathered to watch what was happening.

"Won't someone help us?" asked Dr. Pimento.

No one moved.

Squat laughed. "Her first," he said, pointing to Moomie Peevik. "We'll find someplace very interesting for *her* brain."

"At least I've got one!" said Moomie Peevik.

Four spider-people lifted her into the air.

"Put me down!" she ordered. "You put me down right now!"

They didn't pay any attention.

Blork had had all he could stand. Something new, unlike anything he had ever experienced before, was rumbling deep inside him.

His heart was pounding, and his tongues were quivering.

"YOU PUT HER DOWN!" he belched.

Everyone looked at him in astonishment.

"I SAID: *PUT HER DOWN!*"

The spider-people didn't move.

"Into the ship!" ordered Squat. "Hurry!"

And then it happened. Blork threw the first *poodnoobie* tantrum in the history of the universe. It started small, with a shiver and a shake. Suddenly great howls of rage burst out of his mouth. All three tongues began to flap. He threw himself on the ground screaming and kicking. He bounced off a building and flattened a hovercar.

"YOU PEOPLE ARE DISGUSTING!" he roared with the loudest burp in recorded history.

The cranky people murmured in astonishment.

"YOU SHOULD BE ASHAMED OF YOURSELVES!" he bellowed as he threw Lunk's body this way and that.

The cranky people pressed themselves against the buildings in terror.

"Stop that!" cried Squat. "Stop right now!"

"Remarkable," muttered Dr. Pimento, taking out a notepad.

Lunk stuck his head in a corner and whined.

Moomie Peevik put her hands over Blabber's eyes. "Don't watch," she whispered.

Appus Meko was jumping up and down, shouting, "Go, Blorkie! Go, baby, go!"

His voice was lost in the sound of Blork's mighty belches.

And the tantrum was just getting started.

All the tantrums Blork had held in for the last month—the ones he had not thrown when Appus Meko was bugging him, the ones he had not thrown when Squat kidnapped them, the ones he had not thrown when his brain got moved into Lunk's body—

they all came exploding out in a single mega-neutronic tantrum that made buildings shake, thunder clouds gather, lighting flash.

The pointy-winged creatures that flew above Castle Squat dropped out of the sky and hid in the mountains.

Blork flattened signposts. He made holes in the street.

The spider-people threw themselves to the ground and began to crawl away.

"Come back here, you cowards!" roared Squat. "Come ba-a-a—"

His words were cut short as Blork soared into the air, then landed on top of him.

Blork sighed. He felt better for having the tantrum out of his system.

Suddenly the cranky people began to shout.

Uh-oh, Blork thought. *Sounds like the trouble's not over yet.*

Then he realized what they were saying.

Now what do I do? he thought in horror.

7

BIG
FINISH

Snarf has a new emperor!" cried the cranky people. "We have found someone crankier than Squat! Down with Squat! Up with . . . with . . . the big purple bozo!"

Blork crawled out of the hole he had made in the street.

A tiny voice drifted up from beneath him. "That was some tantrum," said Squat admiringly.

Three of the cranky people crawled in and

lifted him out. He was flatter and shorter than he used to be.

"You are no longer Emperor of Snarf," they told him. "We have found someone crankier to take your job."

"Nuts!" yelled Squat. He threw down his ray gun and stamped on it. Then he crossed his arms and started to pout.

The spider-people scuttled over to Blork. "You are our new boss," they said juicily, bowing down to him. "You are the King of Crankiness!"

Blork was embarrassed. "I'm not *really* crankier than Squat. I just get carried away once in a while. Honest!"

"You sure do," said Appus Meko. "That was fantastic! You're still the best, Blork."

Blork looked at him in astonishment.

"You don't want to be our emperor?"

asked the cranky people in surprise. They sounded angry.

"You wouldn't want me to take the job," said Blork quickly. "I'm really cheerful most of the time. This was just an accident."

"What an accident," said Appus Meko.

"Do you mean we'll have to settle for stinky old Squat?" moaned the cranky people.

"Say yes," begged Squat. "Oh, please please please say yes. I'll have Dr. Pimento put your brain back in your own body. And I'll never bother you again, promise promise promise. Just let me stay in charge here."

Blork thought about it. "How are we supposed to get home?" he asked. "We won't all fit in my space scooter."

"I'll give you my ship," said Squat. "Just let me stay in charge here."

Blork's eyes lit up. All three of his tongues flopped out of his mouth. No kid had ever had a ship like Squat's. If he had that, he could go anywhere in the galaxy.

"Do you want Squat to be your emperor?" he asked the Snarfians.

The cranky people all sighed. "If we have

67

to," they whined. "We never get the good stuff. We always have to settle for second best."

Moomie Peevik came over and whispered in his ear. Her idea was so perfect that Blork accidentally licked her.

Turning back to the cranky people, he said, "All right, here's the deal. I *will* be Emperor of Snarf."

"We have a new boss!" cried the spider-people. "Long live Emperor Blork!"

"Wait, wait," said Blork. "Because I have many other things to do, I appoint Squat to run this place while I'm gone."

He turned to Squat. "That means *I'm* the boss," he said. "The spider people work for me now. Give me any trouble, and you're out of a job."

"Yes, sir, Mr. Space Brat, sir," said Squat.

Blork wasn't sure he could trust Squat. In fact, he was pretty sure that he *couldn't* trust him. But all he wanted to do was get his brain back in his own body and get out of there. "All right, let's go back to the castle," he said. "By the way, from now on it will be

68

called 'Castle Blork.' I am just loaning it to you."

The cranky people grumbled and muttered and walked away.

"Don't mind them," said Dr. Pimento. "They would have been unhappy no matter what you did."

Soon everyone was back in the secret laboratory. Dr. Pimento pointed to Blabber, who was running in circles going "Aroonga Boonga Boonga!"

"I could put your brain inside him for a while," said the doctor hopefully.

"My own body will do just fine, thank you," said Blork.

"I just wanted to see what would happen," said Dr. Pimento. But he didn't press the point. He had Blork and Lunk climb back onto the tables. He put the helmets on their heads. Then he threw the switch.

A terrible crackling sound filled the room.

A minute later Blork sat up. "I'm in my own body!" he cried, looking down at himself.

The spider-people ran over and unstrapped

him. They unstrapped Lunk, very respectfully. Lunk bounded off the table. He shook his head and wiggled his butt. He rolled on his back and paddled all six legs in the air. Then he raced over to Blork and licked his face with all three tongues.

Blork gave Squat his orders for what to do while he was gone. Then everyone from Splat got ready to climb into the big ship.

"Can I come with you?" asked Dr. Pimento. "I don't really belong here anymore."

Blork looked at the ship. It was enormous.

"It might come in handy to have a mad scientist on board," pleaded Dr. Pimento, making his eyes get bigger.

Blork smiled. "Why not? The more the merrier!"

"Yippee!" cried Dr. Pimento. Then he rushed off to get his equipment. The spider-people helped him carry it onto the ship.

"I'm glad I'm staying here," said Squat. "All this sweetness makes me want to puke." He walked away, grumbling as he went.

"All aboard!" cried Blork. "Prepare for blastoff!"

Once everyone was on board, Blork picked up the ship's microphone. "Open the mountain!" he ordered.

The spider-people pulled cranks and levers. The doors in the side of the mountain swung open.

Blork fired up his engines.

"Where are we going, Captain Blork?" asked Appus Meko.

"To the Galactic Celebration! I've still got a medal to accept."

"And after that?" asked Moomie Peevik.

"Home, of course," said Blork.

Then he smiled.

"But I think we'll take the long way back. Our trip has just begun, gang. We've got planets to discover, star systems to span, adventures to . . . uh . . . ."

"Advent?" suggested Moomie Peevik.

"Right!" cried Blork. "Adventures to advent! It's time to see the galaxy!"

The ship soared out of the mountain, and into the starry sky.

"Space Brat and awaaaaay!" cried Blork as he pushed the zoomstick into hyperdrive. "So long Squat—*hello galaxy!*"

DANGER DO NOT TOUCH THIS!

About the Author and Illustrator

BRUCE COVILLE was born in Syracuse, New York. As he was a practically perfect child, it is not possible that the character of Blork is in any way based on his own personality. He first became interested in writing when he was in the sixth grade, and decided to write children's books when he read *Winnie the Pooh* for the first time at the age of nineteen. (He might have read the book sooner, but he couldn't understand it until then.) Mr. Coville lives in Syracuse with his wife, illustrator Katherine Coville, and more pets than are really necessary. He has written nearly four dozen books for children, including *My Teacher Is an Alien, Goblins in the Castle, Aliens Ate My Homework,* and *The Dragonslayers.*

KATHERINE COVILLE is a self-taught artist who is known for her ability to combine finely detailed drawings with a deliciously wacky sense of humor. She is also a toy-maker, specializing in creatures hitherto unseen on this planet. She likes miniatures, and once made a dollhouse inside an acorn. Her other collaborations with Bruce Coville include *The Monster's Ring, The Foolish Giant, Sarah's Unicorn, Goblins in the Castle, Aliens Ate My Homework,* and *The Dragonslayers.*

The Covilles live in a big, old brick house, along with an assortment of odd children, a dog named Booger, and two cats named Spike and Thunder.